How The Pirates

Saved Christmas

James F. and Sarah Jane Kaserman

Manufactured in the United States of America

Library of Congress Catalog Card Number: 2005904195

ISBN: 0-9674081-2-1

Illustrations: Lorrie M. Bennett
Cover design and illustration: Lorrie M. Bennett
Back Cover photo: Kim Freis
Edited by: Pat Clous and Louise Kaserman

Pirate Publishing International
6323 St. Andrews Circle, S.
Fort Myers, FL 33919-1719
(239) 939-4845

IN ORDER
TO UNDERSTAND
OUR FUTURE,
IT IS VITAL THAT WE KNOW
OUR PAST HISTORY,
BOTH REAL AND MYTHICAL.

A WORLD TURNED UPSIDE DOWN

Throughout history it is in difficult times, often during war, that the true spirit of Christmas shines brightly.

The Revolutionary War, which resulted in the forming of the United States of America, was a long and confusing war, lasting from 1775 until 1783. A "world turned upside down" is how most people of the time described the American Revolutionary War. The song "The World Turned Upside Down" was even played by the British at the war's end.

In 1776, only two and one-half million people lived in the United States. One hundred thousand people fought for the Americans and were called "Rebels" or "Patriots". Fifty thousand who wanted to remain true to England fought on the side of the British and were called "Loyalists" or "Tories." The majority of people did not choose one side or the other.

In the Revolutionary War, it was common for brother to fight against brother. Often wives did not agree with their husbands' beliefs. Members of entire families were sometimes torn apart when they had to choose sides in this war. Many of the soldiers and sailors on either side were children.

One cause of the Revolutionary War was taxes that England decided to collect from the American Colonies. These taxes were needed to pay for the expenses of the Seven Years War. That war was fought earlier between England and France on the frontiers of America to protect the American colonies. These taxes were not nearly as high as those paid by the British back in England, but Americans have never liked to pay taxes.

Another cause of the Revolutionary War was a law that England passed which stated that the colonies could trade their goods only with England. The younger colonial merchants could not profit by being allowed to trade only with England. They wanted the freedom to trade with other countries.

The colonists declared their independence from England on July 4, 1776, in Philadelphia, Pennsylvania. At the start of the war, the American colonists had few navy ships. The English navy had thousands of warships and was the largest navy in the world. In order to quickly "grow" a navy, the colonists hired pirates and other private ship owners under a contract called, "A Letter of Marque." There were nearly 1,500 of this mixed group called "privateers" working for the patriots during the American Revolution. Privateering helped the American rebels as well as hurting British shipping because captured cargoes provided them with military supplies. The British also had to use many of their important fighting ships to try to protect their merchant ships.

The Revolutionary War was a bloody and brutal conflict. The guns and rifles had short firing ranges so battles were often decided in hand-to-hand combat with swords and bayonets. The soldiers and sailors were close enough to see and touch their enemy. It was a personal war.

Our story takes place in 1778 during the Revolutionary War and shows how the Christmas spirit is a part of each of us, even during the dark times of war when our whole world seems to be turned upside down.

Somewhere, between real history you have read and stories you may have heard, lies the truth about how a group of pirates, or privateers, led by a dog and a white dolphin, saved Christmas for the children of Savannah, Georgia.

So, come aboard the **AMERICAN DREAM!** Join our crew of privateers as you read the story of "How the Pirates Saved Christmas!"

ONE

PRIVATEER LIFE AT SEA

"People with good ideas have more than one idea. Everyone on this ship must continue to plan new ways to do things."

-CaptainRichards
December 2, 1778

Twelve-year-old Samuel Reed yawned as he rolled from his sleeping hammock. He was careful not to bump the hammock next to his as he ran a hand through his tousled sand-colored hair and rubbed his blue eyes. It was dim and the early morning air smelled of sweat in the crowded sleeping quarters. Only the insistent tugging at his hammock by the ship's cook had awakened him.

Samuel stifled another yawn as he stumbled along behind the cook for the first of his many duties on board the privateer brigantine AMERICAN DREAM. He was one of the youngest members of the crew on the ship, which was now sailing northward off the eastern coast of Florida, and this morning he was needed to help prepare a breakfast of biscuits and salty pork. Samuel sighed as he thought of the supper that would not be much different, with only the addition of peas and maybe potatoes. How he wished for the fresh fruit, vegetables, and fish they had left back in Key West!

After Samuel finished helping the cook, he went back to store the hammocks in the netting that held them out of the way and then made his way up to the deck to wait for further directions. He shivered in the brisk December wind blowing off the Atlantic Ocean as again he longed for the warm, balmy breezes of Key West.

Ever since Samuel had volunteered to serve aboard the ship after his father became ill, he wondered if the money he made was worth the risk. Pirate privateers often chose this way of life because they could earn more money and have more freedom than serving in the regular navy and Samuel's family needed the money.

Despite the danger of being attacked by enemy ships, the days on board the brigantine were often long and boring. There were many daily chores necessary to keep the ship in good condition. The only escape was evening entertainment when the sailors' spirits were charged with story telling, games, whittling, and music.

As Samuel waited for directions from Lieutenant Moses Jackson, he reflected that the crew was lucky to have on board the privateer brigantine an American captain, Captain Charles Richards, who encouraged this sort of entertainment. A band of pirates, hating the restrictions of the British crown, had rescued Captain Richards from the British, who had been forcing him to serve in their navy. He was then given the pirate brigantine to command. After the war against England began in 1776, Captain Richards began to work for the American colonies. He obtained a "letter of marque", or special commission, to capture the cargo of foreign vessels and disrupt British shipping along the North American coast. The pirate brigantine was renamed AMERICAN DREAM and some colonists referred to these paid pirates as "privateers". Other countries, such as England, still considered them pirates.

Samuel jumped, startled, as his thoughts were interrupted by a gruff voice behind him. "Time to begin mending that torn sail," rumbled Lt. Jackson's deep voice. "We'll need all our cloth to overtake a prize merchant vessel," he bellowed.

Samuel was thinking that his prize would be to escape with his life when they met an enemy ship, when another boy joined him on the deck. James Hunter was two years older than Samuel, with dark hair and dark eyes. His job was to repair the sails and work on the rigging of the ship. James had also joined the crew because his family needed the money.

Both boys squatted down to pick up the torn sails when Samuel decided to risk asking Lt. Jackson a question that had been puzzling him. "Sir," he began, "just what kind of cargoes are we searching for on the ships from England, Spain, and Holland that travel to the West Indies islands and the coast of North America?"

"Lad, of course, the colonists need all the ammunition, firearms, and knives they can get from Europe, but they can also use the sugar, molasses, and other products from the West Indies. So, we waylay any ship we can from a foreign port," Lt. Jackson replied as he handed Samuel and James the mending pouch. "Since France has now entered the war against England, the French ships work with us," he added with a surprising twinkle in his black eyes.

Encouraged, James asked, "But if we are plundering ships from other countries, why do we run up their flag on our mast when they are approaching?"

"You think we want them to recognize us for what we are?" laughed the Lieutenant. "That's why we always have a lookout and a variety of flags handy…if they believe we might be a friendly ship, they won't fire first. Therein lies the advantage."

A series of frantic yips interrupted Samuel's next question. The boys whirled around to see Lucky, the frisky ship's dog, stretching up on the bow of the ship. Lucky was a black, tan, and white hound that had been given to Captain Richards along with the pirate ship. She had a friendly disposition and was a favorite with the crew. Edmund Burke, a political writer sailing with the AMERICAN DREAM, called out jokingly, "I'm going to toss that dog to the sharks if she doesn't stop barking. I wonder what's bothering her."

TWO

SAVING ANGEL

"How a person treats an animal tells you about his
heart."
Samuel Reed, young sailor
December 7, 1778

Barking wildly, Lucky leaned against the
bow of the ship, her hindquarters tense and ready
to pounce. She then raced back across the deck
to the stern, only to yelp at the helmsman who
was steering the ship along a group of deserted
barrier islands at the entrance to Biscayne Bay.
Her tail wagged so fast that James and Samuel
laughed thinking that it might fall off. Looking
much like a hound on a hunt, Lucky then charged
back to the bow of the ship and continued her
frenzied barking.

Samuel, James, and Lt. Jackson rushed to
join the crowd of sailors at the front of the ship to
see what had excited the dog.

"Look! What's wrong with it?" cried James,
pointing ahead. On a sandy spit of island, just off
the left side of the bow, lay a small, white dolphin,
which had accidentally or intentionally beached
itself.

"It is unusual for a baby dolphin to be without its mother," Lt. Jackson said. "Bottlenose Dolphins stay with their mothers for a number of years."

"How can we help it?" asked Samuel anxiously.

"If Lucky were the captain, we might stop and send some men out to rescue it. It still appears to be moving," Lt. Jackson replied.

"Sounds like Lucky has the right idea," Captain Richards smiled as he joined the group at the bow's railing.

"But, sir, should we take the time? What use is that fish to us?" growled Manuel Lugo, the burly deck hand. "Will we eat dolphin tonight? Ha! Ha!" Even in the cool breeze, the beads of sweat ran down his head.

"A Bottlenose Dolphin is not a fish. It is a mammal just like you, Lugo. The only difference is that many people think dolphins are smarter than humans," Captain Richards laughed and winked at Lugo. He turned and shouted, "Bring the ship around! Prepare the ship's boat for launching."

Samuel and James hurried with the others to ready the ship's boat, a small boat attached to the side. It could be either sailed or rowed and provided transportation to and from the "Mother Ship".

James and Samuel hastily handed the oars to the large men assigned to row the ship's boat, and it was lowered over the starboard side. Lucky, propelled by her wagging tail, leaped into the boat as it was lowered. She wanted to command the rescue.

7

"Everything we need to know about life can be learned from a dog," Captain Richards said to the group.

"Nonsense! I have never in my life sailed with such a captain," Lugo spat out as he grabbed the rope in his thick hands.

Lt. Jackson clapped his large hand on Lugo's shoulder and said loudly, "Dogs are man's best friend because they wag their tails instead of their tongues!"

When the eight men and Lucky reached the beach, they immediately began to splash water on the dolphin's skin, which was beginning to look rigid.

Lucky cautiously licked the dolphin near its snout and as they looked into each other's eyes, they both began making whimpering sounds.

The men dragged the little white dolphin into the cool ocean water with Lucky yipping at their heels. As if a switch had been turned on, the young mammal began to move its flukes and flippers. Moving by itself, it swam closer to Lucky who was immersed in the water. Only her head and tail were showing.

"Looks like our ship's dog has a friend," chuckled Solomon Friedman, an older sailor who was an accomplished helmsman.

"That dolphin is lucky," another sailor added, "to be rescued by a dog named Lucky."

With Lucky proudly perched at the bow, the little boat returned through the chalky foam of the water to triumphant cheers from the AMERICAN DREAM. The dolphin could be seen swimming alongside the grinning sailors.

"It appears as if we have gained a crewmember," Lt. Jackson joked.

"Well, there have been many sailors' tales that tell how dolphins have befriended and helped those who live upon the sea," Captain Richards stated.

The AMERICAN DREAM turned and headed north while a white dolphin and a black, tan, and white dog formed a unique masthead.

THREE

FIRST BATTLE AT SEA

"Always listen... most do not. You will learn much if you only listen."
Lt. Moses Jackson
December 10, 1778

Samuel winced as he limped up to the deck, a splinter from the wooden deck embedded in his bare left foot. He shivered in the chilly morning air and wondered what would keep him warm as the AMERICAN DREAM continued north.

Anxiously, hurrying as fast as he could, Samuel joined James at the bow of the ship to see if the dolphin was still traveling with them. For the past three days, the sailors had watched with amusement as it circled the ship. They fed the little mammal small fish while Lucky ran back and forth on the deck, barking approval when the dolphin leaped in the air and slapped its flukes on the surface of the water.

As James pointed out the dolphin, still following the ship, Lt. Jackson's booming voice interrupted Samuel's thoughts. "Hey, lads, don't just stand there! There are decks to be mopped and rigging to be repaired."

Samuel and James guiltily jerked around with their eyes downcast and James stammered an apology. "I'm sorry, sir, but I never saw a such a creature like the dolphin before. I was just wondering why it is following us and not with other dolphins."

Lt. Jackson's kindness shone through his gruff exterior when he took time to answer. "Since it is a young dolphin, perhaps something happened to its mother." He continued, "Dolphins are intelligent, usually good-natured, and playful. They even practice teamwork when they hunt for food. Sometimes, however, they can be clever and even mean when dealing with other dolphins. They may charge, slap each other with their tails, and shove. The pod must have rejected our young dolphin for some reason, perhaps because it was different. I guess we're its family now." Lt. Jackson shrugged and motioned toward the mop while he returned to search the waters for an enemy ship.

The AMERICAN DREAM was still traveling North, now about two-thirds the way up the Florida coast and about five miles from the shore. Though Florida currently belonged to the British crown, it was sparsely populated. Therefore there were not many British troops located there.

The privateer brigantine was, however, sailing in waters that were in the triangular trade route between England, the British West Indies, and the American colonies. The British Navy had deployed many ships to not only defend their shipping lanes, but also to prevent any other nation's ships from delivering goods to either the colonies or the islands of the West Indies.

A sudden shout from the lookout perched high in the ship's rigging caused both Samuel and James to fling down their mops. "A British war ship escorting a merchant ship!" Captain Richards yelled. "Get the British Union Jack flag out and run it up the mast", he commanded.

After the AMERICAN DREAM came abreast of the enemy warship, Captain Richards ordered the British Union Jack flag taken down and the pirate flag hoisted in its place. He had decided to attack the larger warship in order to capture the merchant ship as a prize. The decks were cleared, the ammunition and small arms brought up, and the guns loaded and ready to fire.

Samuel and James were hurrying up with a final load of gunpowder when James was horrified to realize that Lucky was still on the deck! Throwing down his load, he grabbed the excited dog and shoved her down the stairway just before the hatches were closed and sealed.

As the two ships closed on one another, the calm sunshine of the day was disrupted with puffs of acrid-smelling smoke. Loud bangs rang out as the long guns fired upon one another. The blasting of the cannon caused the little dolphin to dive deep into the waves.

"We are a smaller vessel and must make each shot count," Captain Richards yelled. "Aim well my lads, for the future of this day belongs to you."

"We must risk our safety and get closer if we wish to win," Lt. Jackson shouted to Captain Richards.

"We will attack the ship's stern and ram her from behind! Our bowsprit will entangle the rigging of our ship on her. Then, men, throw grappling hooks and we can board," Captain Richards commanded his officers and crew.

"Have the boys bring out their drums to beat the charge," Lt. Jackson ordered.

Manuel Ortiz, a Spanish sailor, thrust a drum at Samuel as James left to help carry ammunition.

"But I have never beat a drum charge," Samuel protested.

"You must learn quickly. This will help to keep you from dying at too young an age," the crusty old Spaniard retorted. "Beat the drums. We are ready to attack!"

Samuel's heart thudded as loudly as his drum when the crack of small arms fire rang out from both sides. Then came the clash of steel on steel as swords and cutlasses were used to subdue the enemy ship. The battle lasted over an hour as smoke, screams, and the smells of battle filled the air.

Samuel's arms and hands were quivering with fear and they ached from beating the drum, but he forced himself to keep on drumming, afraid to quit until ordered to stop.

Finally, the crew lowered the English flags from both captured ships and raised the pirate flags. The battle was over and the AMERICAN DREAM had claimed its first prize as a privateer ship. Eighty-four British sailors had been captured along with fourteen 12-pound cannons and a huge 32-pound cannon on a swivel.

Captain Richards strutted around the deck as he congratulated his crew. "This captured warship will serve the American cause well. We shall escort it and the merchant vessel to Charles Town to sell and we will divide the prize," he exclaimed, as his blue eyes gleamed.

After confining the captured sailors, the members of the crew began singing. The rhythm sparked the men and, fueled by the win, they quickly began to repair the rigging of both ships.

After the horrors of the battle, it was a relief to James to open the hatches and watch Lucky spring back up on deck to rejoin her human shipmates.

"Ahoy, off our starboard, our little friend is back!" shouted the lookout. Lucky and some of the other sailors ran to the railing to see the white form surfacing in the deepening dusk.

"It's like a guardian angel watching over us," murmured James.

FOUR

THE STARS AND STRIPES

"Secrets are worse than letting out the truth!"
French Admiral La Motte Piquet
December 13, 1778

The optimism and enthusiasm of the victory lessened as the crew realized they had to still avoid the enemy by sailing dangerously close to the coasts of Florida and Georgia. Since they were so near, Captain Richards decided to land on one of the many Golden Isles that stretch up the coast of Georgia and into South Carolina in order to repair battle damage.

Samuel joined James at the bow to view the live oaks with their cobweb of Spanish moss. Only winged creatures flying overhead disturbed the mixture of palmetto trees, hardwoods, and towering pine trees. The ship's carpenters would repair the hulls of the ships with this wood.

While some of the crew were cutting the wood and making repairs, Samuel had an idea. "Let's go to the other side of the island to hunt for fish and shellfish so we won't have to eat salt pork again tonight," he said to a few other boys.

After catching as much as they could carry, the boys returned and the three ships sailed with the evening tide. At last they had an escape from the mosquitoes that had attacked them throughout the day. They decided that tramping through the saltwater marshes all day had been too great a price to pay for a savory alternative.

As the first rays of sunlight sparkled on the horizon, the lookout shouted a warning when he spied a squadron of French warships escorting a fleet of merchant ships off to the East. James, who was standing nearby, felt a wave of apprehension grip him as he recalled the fierce battle of three days before.

"Run up the French flags," Captain Richards called out to the sailors now fully awake on the three ships. The crew resembled a bustling ant hill as they frantically obeyed the order.

"Sir, our captured British ships have only their own flag on board and our pirate flags," Lt. Jackson shouted back to Captain Richards.

It was too late. The French flagship, the *Robuste*, fired a warning shot off the bow of the AMERICANDREAM. This shot signaled the smaller fleet to stop and prepare to be boarded.

Within an hour, a longboat appeared from the *Robuste* to take Captain Richards and

Lt. Moses Jackson to its flagship. The crew of the AMERICAN DREAM waited nervously, afraid that though France was an ally, the French Admiral,

not knowing their true identity, would treat them as criminals.

The two Americans were escorted to the Admiral's quarters in the forecastle that lay at the stern of the French Man-of-War. Both men were in awe as they entered the elegant room.

Admiral La Motte Piquet, one of the most respected commanders in the French Navy, began speaking in an icy voice. "I assume you have brought your Letter of Marque if you are legitimate privateers...and if you are, why are you flying a pirate flag?"

As Captain Richards presented the documents to the Admiral, he replied firmly and without hesitation, "Your Excellency, we have just captured two of our vessels from the British. We fight for the Americans but they have not provided us with a flag."

Piquet finally showed a tight smile as he walked around the grand desk in the center of the room.

"The Americans are strange people. They declare their independence from England with no navy and only small, poorly trained state militias. They have no money and no way of making any money." Piquet paused. "But, they have a great amount of courage and a love of liberty that the French people can appreciate."

Piquet quickly turned and went to an ornate table to pick up a folded flag.

"Did you know the Americans now have a flag?" Piquet asked the two men.

"Do you mean the Grand Union Flag, sir?" Moses Jackson questioned.

"No, No, No," Piquet laughed. "Your John Paul Jones gave me this flag last year off the coast of France where we were awaiting a convoy of merchantmen bound for America."

"Why it has stars and stripes!" Captain Richards exclaimed. "Seven red stripes and six white and a blue square with a circle of thirteen white stars."

"Yes, your Captain Jones wanted to exchange a salute with my fleet. He sent me a message, stating that he would fire thirteen guns, one for each star, and wanted me to return gun for gun." Piquet paused and smiled to his other officers. "I sent him a message back that it is a French tradition to fire only nine guns. I guess he decided that nine guns are better than none!" Piquet laughed out loud.

"That must have been the first time the stars and stripes was given recognition by a foreign government," Captain Richards remarked.

"It probably is..." Piquet pondered, "Now, take this flag back to your ships and have your crew sew up similar flags for each vessel. If I catch you in the future without your stars and stripes, I can assure you ninety guns will be fired upon you, and not as a salute!" Admiral Piquet warned the two Americans.

While the French oarsmen rowed back to the AMERICAN DREAM, the little white dolphin seemed to swim in cadence with their oars.

After his crew and Lucky greeted Captain Richards, relieved to see him back safely, he shouted, "James Hunter, front and center!"

James scurried down the ratlines from the main mast and, with his stomach churning nervously, ran to stand meekly in front of the captain.

"Young James, you are a most capable sailor and stitch wonders on our sailcloth. I now want you to find red, white, and blue cloth and sew three flags exactly like this one." The Captain handed him the folded Stars and Stripes he had brought back from the French Admiral.

James, Samuel, and the other boys hurried below deck to take apart the British Union Jack flags in order to sew the new ones.

"If we are to fight for these United States, then we must be willing to carry her banner," Captain Richards announced to the crews of the three ships.

As the three American ships began to weigh anchor, nine loud blasts from the cannon of the *Robuste* roared out in salute.

Captain Richards ordered his gunners to return a thirteen-gun salute.

Under billowing sails, the Americans continued north and the French fleet continued southeast, the crews waving good-bye and yelling encouragement to one another. Lucky's barks joined the shouts and soon the white dolphin was spotted again jumping out of the water, now that the shooting was over.

FIVE

BECOMING SPIES

"As soon as a moment passes, it is history."

James Hunter
December 15, 1778

The boys stitched into the night, their hands tingling and cramped with the repetition of pushing the needle in and out of the coarse material. As Samuel rubbed his eyes, tired of squinting in the dim lamplight, he suddenly felt homesick when he remembered how his mother would stitch into the darkness to make his Christmas gifts. Without thinking, he blurted out, "I wish I could be back home with my family for Christmas."

After a few silent seconds, James replied quietly, "It won't be the same without our families to share this special time, but everyone on this ship is going to be a member of our Christmas family. We will need to think how we can make it special for them.

After forty hours had passed, the boys were exhausted, having had only a few hours of sleep, but the flags were finished. Despite their tiredness, the young pack beamed with pride as they handed the flags carefully to the captain.

"These flags are superior to the one given us by Admiral Piquet!" Captain Richards exclaimed.

"Thank you, sir," James replied as he stretched his stiff fingers. "Lucky helped, too. A wet nose is a worthy taskmaster when one wants to stop and rest."

"Yes, but Lucky slept after she was sure we were awake and working," Samuel added.

"You are quite an artist, young James," Captain Richards praised. "I am glad that we finally have these banners since they were approved on June 14, 1777. You would think that the Continental Congress would have provided us with flags by now."

"Sir, these are indeed difficult times for the thirteen colonies," Lt. Jackson gently reminded him.

"The fact is that, thanks to you lads, we shall now be able to fly the national flag on all three ships as we continue our sail to Charles Town," Captain Richards stated. Then he shook each boy's weary hand firmly. This exchange was rare given the difference in rank.

"Perhaps we should stop by Beaufort, first.

If we anchor in Port Royal Sound, we can gather the latest news and enter Charles Town safely," Lt. Jackson suggested.

"Fine idea," Captain Richards decided. "Send our most literate sailors ashore so that they can read the broadsides and the South Carolina Gazette. Instruct them to converse with fellow patriots to insure our safety in going on to Charles Town. Also, they can find out about the sandbars which may block the entrance to Charles Town."

"What are broadsides? I thought that was only a navy term," a yawning Samuel asked, without stopping to think that he had spoken out of turn.

"Broadsides are posters nailed to trees and fence posts. They have news printed on them and many times they are also used to recruit new soldiers and sailors. By reading them we can find out what has been happening," Captain Richards answered.

Lt. Jackson added, "All those going ashore, listen to the town crier who shouts out the news to those who cannot read. That will give us more recent information. Talk to the Patriots who can warn us of any potential dangers."

"How will they know friend or foe...a Patriot from a Loyalist?" James asked with a puzzled look.

"They must be extremely cautious. The Loyalists are the eyes and ears of our enemy. If asked what they eat or drink, our men are being tested to see if they are fellow Loyalists. Loyalists identify each other by answering that they drink tea," Captain Richards replied.

"Then how will they know a Patriot?" Samuel burst out.

"Most towns, like Beaufort, have committees of safety. If they can manage to find a member of the committee who trusts them, they can come into the circle of the true Patriots," Captain Richards replied.

He added, "The number thirteen is important to the Patriots since there are thirteen colonies. When you approach someone whom you think may be a Patriot, try to use this as a signal to identify yourself as a fellow Patriot."

"Does this mean we will be going ashore? James asked, his eyes widening with interest.

"Yes, I am sending you two along with two of the older sailors and even Lucky ashore. Your ability to read and think is important to our mission. Two boys with a dog and two old men asking questions should not arouse too much suspicion," Captain Richards surmised. "Now get some sleep. You will need your wits about you."

As day passed into night, three ships, flying the Stars and Stripes, quietly slipped from the Atlantic Ocean into Port Royal Sound.

The moonlight danced on the water. The outer lights of Beaufort served as a beacon as the ship's boat, carrying the four sailors and Lucky on the bow, silently followed their little dolphin guide into the darkness and potential danger.

SIX

HISTORIC CHARLESTOWN, S.C.

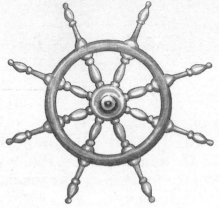

"It is amazing that stupid people know the answers to almost anything while smart people question or doubt almost everything."

Lt. Moses Jackson
December 19, 1778

As the ship's boat bobbed up and down in the choppy, gray water on its return to the AMERICAN DREAM the next afternoon, Captain Richards was seen pacing back and forth along the deck. His look of relief on seeing that the four sailors were back safely was replaced with a worried look as he asked anxiously, "What's the news?"

James quickly answered, "The British know that Charles Town is an important port to our cause. They have many of their own navy ships and British privateers trying to blockade the entrance to the harbor so supplies from the northern colonies and from the French cannot get in. Another problem is that the harbor is shallow. We must be careful entering the city to avoid both the British privateers and the treacherous sandbars that could cement our three ships to the ocean floor."

"That confirms our suspicions," Captain Richards said pensively as Lt. Jackson joined them. "But, if we are to sell our prizes, we must run the blockade! What else did you learn?" he continued.

"The British appear to be focusing their war efforts on capturing Charles Town and Savannah," Samuel added. "It is crucial that we avoid their frigates," he said confidently in his self-appointed position as a strategist.

"Last year, British frigates were successful in sinking American as well as French ships near Long Island and Sullivan's Island," Lt. Jackson interrupted. "One surprise turn of events could finish us!"

"Well, if we are to collect money for our prizes we have to sail into Charles Town. Sailing further north this time of year is not an option. Besides the bad weather, we would have to avoid British ships and privateers to get into northern harbors as well," Captain Richards decided.

"Our share of the prizes will be most welcome since we are only a week from Christmas," James stated, thinking of a belated celebration with his family back in Florida.

"Anything else?" Captain Richards asked the group.

"The Patriots in Beaufort at first thought we were 'cowboys', Samuel laughed.

"What do you mean, 'cowboys'?" Lt. Jackson asked.

"It is said the English Loyalists ring cowbells to attract people into a woods or pasture, then they rob them," Samuel answered.

"Or, they steal farm animals, mostly cows, and then sell them to the British army," James added.

"I wonder what they call Patriot outlaws?" Lt. Moses chuckled.

"I know," James shouted. "They call them 'skinners'."

"Skinners?" Moses asked doubtfully.

"Yes, the Patriot outlaws take all of a Loyalist's belongings, leaving him only with his bare skin!"

There was a chorus of laughter as the three ships started sailing to the north towards Charles Town with the crew optimistically hoping for good weather and an absence of British ships.

The weather, however, turned colder the next morning as a front moved from the northwest through Charles Town and into the Atlantic. The sky was a sullen gray color and the waves grew large as the three ships neared the entrance to Charles Town harbor.

Lucky barked steadily while the bow of the AMERICAN DREAM rose and fell in a frightening cadence, sending crashing waves across the decks. As she somehow kept her balance against the railing, Seaman Solomon Friedman, who was clutching the wheel, exclaimed, "That dog looks like she's trying to talk to the little dolphin!"

"I think the dolphin is trying to guide us away from the shallows," Lt. Jackson shouted to Captain Richards.

"Try to keep the dolphin in sight and follow it," Captain Richards yelled to Solomon as a cold rain began to fall.

As he gave his orders, a British frigate appeared through the mist. As they followed the dolphin safely across the Cape Fear sandbar, they could see the British ship run aground only a few yards from the place where the dolphin had guided the three ships.

As the crew realized how perilously close they had come to destruction, Lt. Jackson exclaimed, "That dolphin saved us. It is indeed our guardian angel!"

The three ships continued into Charles Town harbor with the little white dolphin acting as a harbor pilot.

SEVEN

CONFUSION IN CHARLESTOWN

"As long as we live there will be troubles to contend
with and difficult decisions to make."

Lt. Moses Jackson
December 20, 1778

After guiding the three ships safely into
Charles Town Harbor to the Cooper River, "Angel",
newly named by the privateers, disappeared into
the fog.

From the Cooper River, the ships traveled
up the Wando River and reached Hobcaw Creek.
The crew had to navigate through the mouth of
Hobcaw Creek to reach the Pritchard Shipyard.
The cold wind and light rain continued as they
worked to berth the ships. The shipyard, in the
gray light, resembled a shabby overcoat that had
been laid aside. Shivering and jerking with every

sneeze, Samuel helped James as they slipped and struggled up the rope ladders to stow the sail.

"After we dock our ships, we must decide to whom we will sell," Captain Richards informed his crew. "We have a choice. We can sell the ships to either the State Navy of South Carolina or to the Continental Navy," he explained. "Each will try to pay us with their nearly worthless currency."

"Or," Captain Richards paused, "we might sell to private citizens who will pay us in gold or land. But, no matter to whom we sell the ships, those in the State Navy or the Continental Navy will dislike us."

"Why should they dislike us?" Manuel Lugo challenged.

"Well, Captain Richards went on, "since both the state of South Carolina and the Continental Congress are deeply in debt, their money is nearly worthless. It is with those worthless bills that the navies are paid. As privateers, we will demand our payment in gold and silver, provisions, or land. This means that we are making more money than the sailors of either navy. This problem has caused the number of privateers to grow and the navies to grow short on manpower. Just look around you. The unkempt condition of this shipyard proves my point," Captain Richards smiled.

After securing the two prize ships, the privateer sailors who had sailed on the other two ships boarded the AMERICAN DREAM to sail back to the city of Charles Town. At once they were enthusiastically greeted by Lucky racing around the deck.

As the sun dispelled the gray clouds, Samuel asked wistfully, "Do you think we will be spending Christmas in Charles Town? Since we can't be home, it would be much nicer in town than out on the cold Atlantic Ocean."

Looking thoughtful, James replied, "I don't know, but let's take Lucky with us to explore. Maybe we can think of a way to make Christmas special for the crew if we stay here."

With the last docking chore completed, the boys hurried down the gangplank, anxious to get off the bobbing vessel and feel solid ground under their feet.

While Captain Richards and the other officers went to gather any information to promote their impending sale, the rest of the crew left to relax and enjoy shore time.

Most of the men eagerly made their way to the Pink House, a simple tavern where they could drink grog and smoke. This house was nestled among an area of small houses and not an attraction to the two excited boys. Their quest lay in the discovery of a real city.

"These streets are made of stones and are not sandy like those back home," Samuel exclaimed as they walked towards the tall Customs and Exchange building.

"Lt. Jackson told me about these cobblestones. They were used as a ballast by many ships to help them keep their balance. The stones were left here and replaced with cargo when the ships returned to England," James replied.

As they passed the Dock Street Theater, though their stomachs were beginning to rumble with hunger, the boys were still too excited to take time to find food. "I'm glad we don't waste time sitting around and smoking like the others," Samuel blurted out.

"I agree. They have to go to a second floor long room to blow smoke at each other since it's illegal for men to be seen smoking by a woman," James laughed. "What a waste of a beautiful day just to get a face full of smoke."

As the sun began to cast long shadows, Samuel and James finally gave in to their hunger and found a friendly tavern where they ate a hearty meal of oysters before returning to the ship.

Early the next morning, Captain Richards called the crew on the deck to share the offers received in Charles Town. After much discussion, they voted to sell the merchant ship to a private merchant in Charles Town for gold and silver. Each sailor would receive a Spanish gold doubloon and some silver pieces of eight.

"Samuel, a gold doubloon is worth seven weeks pay to an ordinary seaman!" James exclaimed after doing some quick figuring.

The captured British warship was sold to a Continental Congress representative in exchange for grants of land with deeds for each sailor. The older sailors had argued for money, but the younger sailors were excited to own land at such a young age.

To complete the deal, the representative had also agreed to provide provisions and ammunition to resupply the AMERICAN DREAM.

With business affairs over, Lt. Jackson abruptly changed the subject by asking, "Are we staying in Charles Town for Christmas, sir?"

Heads jerked up as all froze, waiting anxiously to hear the answer.

"As appealing as it might be to stay here and feast, we must learn from our enemy about too much revelry at Christmas," Captain Richards cautioned. "Remember what General Washington and his Continental Army did to the Hessians on Christmas of 1776. We are on guard and safer at sea where we can defend ourselves than here in a city the British are intent upon capturing."

Sulking, the crew resumed loading the AMERICAN DREAM with new provisions and ammunition. Seeing the boys' dejected looks, Lt. Jackson tried to explain Captain Richards' decision. "Throughout life we can expect to have to make difficult decisions. Our captain is willing to make these decisions which is the reason that we elected him our captain."

With the afternoon tide of December 21, 1778, the AMERICAN DREAM sailed down the Cooper River to leave the city of Charles Town and Christmas behind.

EIGHT

A CHRISTMAS PRESENT FROM THE SEA

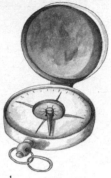

"There are countless stories about animals who save people. We need to try and better understand animals."

Lt. Moses Jackson
December 23, 1778

With the outgoing tide, Angel again led the **AMERICANDREAM** through the dangerous shallow water. Manuel Lugo and a few of the crew still grumbled about the Captain actually following a "fish", while Lucky barked from the bow.

"Lieutenant Jackson, don't you wonder about our captain following a dolphin?" Samuel asked earnestly as he and James watched from the side.

"There are many stories about wild animals befriending humans. I have talked to older sailors who tell stories about dolphins that have saved their ships and led them away from danger."

"But, it just seems so strange," Samuel insisted.

"Well, sometimes those who listen to animals are not so fortunate," Lt. Jackson warned. He began to tell the story of an American general, Charles Lee, who served with General Washington earlier in the year. "General Lee is a strange man who prefers talking to dogs rather than talking to humans. Unfortunately, he suffered defeat in June by the British and was relieved of his command by General Washington."

"Where is he now?" James asked.

"Last I heard, he was alone and still talking to his dogs," he laughed as he saw the boys' mouths drop open.

At that moment, Angel abruptly turned toward one of the nearby barrier islands. Over the gentle slapping of the waves on the hull and the flapping of the sails, the sounds of violin music drifted in the light wind.

"Ship aground on Long Island! Looks to be French," came a yell from the crow's nest.

The crew of the AMERICAN DREAM looked in the direction of the floundering ship. Angel's interest had overcome her guide duty as she changed directions.

"She's a big ship, looks to be four hundred tons," the lookout shouted down to the Captain.

"All sailors to their battle stations." came the alarmed shout from Captain Richards, "The music may be a trap."

41

With a thrill of excitement, James and Samuel sprang to their assigned posts. As Samuel retrieved his drum, he wished he could join James who was scrambling up the ratlines to his shaky perch among the sails.

"Lookout, tell us what you see," Captain Richards called urgently from the deck.

"Aye, sir. I see no sails or mast. It looks as if she has run aground on the beach," came the report from the lookout above. "There are no crew that I can see; but it appears that there are a woman and a girl on their ship's forecastle waving at us."

"Captain, we must rescue them," insisted Lt. Jackson.

"Not so fast," cautioned Captain Richards, "we do not want to fall victim to one of our own pirate tricks. How many times have we masqueraded as innocent travelers but with pistol and cutlass hidden beneath our clothes? Then we waited until some unsuspecting ship attempted to rescue us so we could attack and capture them and their ship."

"Shall we stand off ready to fire and send only a boarding party to them until we are sure?" asked Lt. Jackson.

"Yes, load the cannon and prepare to fire a broadside in case this is a trick," Captain Richards commanded. "Take eight of our crew in the ship's boat and investigate."

Lowering the ship's boat and rowing to the stricken vessel took nearly an hour. Meanwhile, the sailors on board the AMERICANDREAM watched with apprehension through the afternoon shadows to see the outcome. All the while, the sweet sounds of Christmas carols and hymns from the stricken ship broke the silence.

Lt. Jackson, commanding the ship's boat, ordered it to the beach a safe distance from the stranded ship. Captain Richards commented, "Lt. Jackson is a wise warrior. Take heed. Too many people lose their lives in battle because they rush directly into the enemy's plan."

When Lieutenant Jackson's men decided that it looked safe and began to climb the side of the French merchant vessel, Captain Richards ordered a warning shot be fired from his cannon into the Atlantic. This was to signal to those on the French ship that they should surrender or be destroyed.

Shortly after, a lantern signal from Lt. Jackson indicated that the stricken ship was secure. Captain Richards ordered his men to "stand down" from their battle stations and to prepare to move the AMERICAN DREAM closer.

As the AMERICAN DREAM neared the French vessel, Captain Richards leaned over the side to shout, "It isn't often that the British leave us a ship to be claimed as a prize."

"Perhaps it is their Christmas present to us," Lt. Jackson yelled back, "although we haven't checked for cargo yet. The only people aboard seem to be the woman and a girl!"

NINE

TO CHOOSE THE GREATER GOOD

"Sometimes we have to decide between good and a greater good."

Captain Richards
December 22, 1778

After the **AMERICANDREAM** had drawn close, the ship's boat brought over the two passengers and the crew helped them climb the rope ladder to board. The shawls covering their long woolen skirts and bodices provided little warmth, as they still shivered in the cold. The woman was tall, with expressive dark eyes. The girl, who looked about 12 years old, had brown eyes and clutched a violin case.

In the dusk, as Captain Richards approached the pair trying to remember what he knew of the French language, he was astonished when the lady said in English, "I cannot thank you enough for rescuing us. My daughter and I would surely have perished in the cold."

Captain Richards soon found out that the British had captured the crew of the French ship two days before. They had then scuttled the ship while the woman and girl hid among the sleeping hammocks. After he had ordered warm drinks and food for his new passengers, the captain took them to his quarters where they all sat down at his large map table. In the lighted cabin, he could now see that the woman had dark brown hair with reddish glints. The girl's hair was a warm brown.

After Captain Richards had introduced himself, he began his questioning by asking, "Who are you and why were you on a French ship if you speak English?"

The dark haired figure appeared uneasy as she eyed the captain. Softly she answered. "My name is Louise Melbourne. My daughter, Sarah, and I are from the British island of Saint Christopher, better known as St. Kitts, in the Caribbean Ocean. My husband, who was an overseer on a large sugar plantation, died from a fever he contracted from the slaves in his charge four years ago. When the Revolution in the American colonies began, the French and Spanish navies broke the supply lines to our island. No grain or flour from the colonies could reach us. Thousands on our island are starving. Sarah and I needed to escape and find our way to my brother's home in South Carolina or we would perish also."

Sarah finally put down her violin case and daringly added, "I am so excited to finally meet my Uncle James and Aunt Shannon. They have a small farm that they work by themselves. Uncle James Randolph is a Patriot who is away fighting in the Revolution and we are going to help Aunt Shannon run the farm."

The aroma of the food interrupted them, and even the standard salt pork and potatoes were tempting as Louise and Sarah hungrily began to eat.

When they finished, the captain continued, "How did you get to St. Kitts if your family is from South Carolina?"

Louise answered confidently, "I met my husband when he was visiting Charles Town to arrange for a rice shipment to his island. It was a chance encounter. We wrote to each other often and finally I agreed to go to St. Kitt's to marry him. Never did I realize the sad slavery situation that existed there. Furthermore, I did not know how much I would miss my family and South Carolina."

Captain Richards looked confused as he persisted, "How did you manage to gain passage on a French ship? Since France and England are at war, it could not possibly land at St. Kitts."

Louise explained, "I used money I had saved to pay a sympathetic friend to sail us to St. Martin, a French island, on a small sloop. Then the rest of the money paid our passage on this ship, which had stopped there. We were part of a cargo of molasses, sugar, and coffee bound for the colonies. The rest of the cargo was gunpowder and firearms from France as well as some little valuables for the wealthier citizens of Charles Town. If it were possible, I would pay you for your trouble, but all we have left is our clothes and Sarah's violin, so we cannot pay you to transport us. Sarah and I are, however, very capable with cooking and sewing and she has a special talent with her violin.

Just then, there was a knock on the door and Lt. Jackson entered to report, "Captain, the French ship is of no value to us! All that the British left on the ship are some boxes of linen and china, and a store of children's tea sets, dolls, toy soldiers, marbles, tops, and games. They must have been Christmas presents heading for the citizens of Charles Town who could afford them."

Louise and Sarah followed Captain Richards up to the dark deck, where the crew waited for directions. The oil lantern lights were no match for a night at sea.

"It would appear that the British have taken all cargo of any value from the ship," Captain Richards announced to the crew. "It is your decision to either destroy the ship or let it remain here."

"Or, we could tow the ship into Charles Town and deliver the toys and gifts to those for whom they were intended," James said aloud while standing before the crew.

"That is a foolish suggestion!" Manuel Lugo shouted back. "We have just left Charles Town.

You know how much trouble we had getting into the harbor. The British will be patrolling to look for any ship going there. You are the one who told Captain Richards that you overheard British attack plans. I vote we leave the ship where it is and rid ourselves of the women as soon as possible," he argued.

The crew fractured in boisterous groups. Each discussed the problem and argued the solutions.

"Well, why not tow the ship and give the cargo to the children and Patriots in Savannah," James suggested. "After all, it is on our way back to either Florida or the West Indies, wherever we decide to head."

"Why in the world are you so intent on doing a good deed?" Hugo snapped at James.

"Because Christmas is near and this war has lasted so long," James answered. "It would be rewarding to bring some joy into the Patriots' lives and also into ours."

Perhaps hearing the sweet Christmas carols on the violin earlier during the day had put many of the crew in the Christmas spirit. When the vote was called, more than half the men agreed to tow the French ship, with the gifts aboard, on to Savannah, Georgia.

Sarah, stepping out of the Captain's cabin, approached James and said softly, "James, I felt so sad, thinking that all those gifts were going to sink to the bottom of the ocean." She touched her hand on his arm.

"You must never let others control your feelings," James said with a smile.

"You are a good-hearted person, and you make me happy." Sarah grinned, and without warning, leaned over to kiss him on the cheek.

Samuel, when he saw the kiss, announced to everyone that a girl had kissed James. Laughter rippled among the crew, releasing the tension that the vote had created.

The next morning, as the two vessels headed south toward Savannah, Lt. Jackson patted Captain Richards on the back. "Sometimes deciding between doing the right thing and not doing the right thing can be quite difficult," he said.

Captain Richards replied, "Many times we must decide between a good and bad choice yet, sometimes we have to decide between good and a greater good."

"Maybe that's what will make this Christmas special for us," James quietly added.

Gleeful yips from Lucky interrupted the moment as she spotted Angel once again guiding the two ships safely southward.

"Keep following the dolphin," Captain Richards said to Lt. Jackson. "Boys, you got your wish," he added with a wink. "You will be spending Christmas in a city. I hope the citizens of Savannah will appreciate the gifts we are bringing them."

TEN

THE TRUE SPIRIT OF CHRISTMAS

"A dog like Lucky can teach us what the spirit of Christmas should be, to love others more than we love ourselves."
-Captain Richards
Christmas Day, December 25, 1778

The next morning, as the AMERICAN DREAM continued to tow the stricken French ship south, the lookout suddenly shouted, "Off to the starboard...a British frigate!"

Instantly Captain Richards alerted the men: "Battle stations!" As the crew rushed to their fighting posts, he fixed his glass on the newcomer. The British warship was none other than the fearful 32-gun *Brune* under the command of Captain Ferguson. The *Brune* had a notorious reputation for sending many of its victims to the bottom of the sea during the past year.

"Captain Ferguson is a dangerous man and deals terror to our navy," Captain Richards exclaimed, as they waited for the expected cannon fire. Incredibly, the British ship veered instead and sailed southeast into the Atlantic Ocean away from the two ships.

"Captain Ferguson would never let an opportunity to attack us pass," Captain Richards warned Lt. Moses. "There is something suspicious going on that we don't know about. Rather than get trapped in Savannah, we will put our ship's boat ashore on Tybee Island beach near the lighthouse and send someone to Mud Fort to be sure the Americans are still in control."

At first light on Christmas Eve morning, the ghostly shape of Tybee Island was in view. James and Samuel were ordered to take Lucky when they went ashore to find out if it were safe to go on into the port city. "Two boys and a mongrel look innocent," Captain Richards smiled. "None of them looks like a spy."

After being rowed to Tybee Island by two crew members, the boys and Lucky checked inside the lighthouse keeper's cabin. Finding it deserted, they walked inland many miles along the riverbank to the earthen fortification that was called "Mud Fort". Its strategic location along the bank of the Savannah River insured that no ship could gain access to the city without passing it. The walls of Mud Fort were fortified with cannon that could destroy ships in the narrow Savannah River.

53

Mud Fort had been abandoned several months earlier because of disease among the troops. Now reopened by the Patriots, there were only a small number of troops stationed there. Samuel and James sprinted inside the walls and hurried to the commanding officer to tell him about the *Brune*. They were relieved when he loudly proclaimed, "No ship will slip past us successfully and attack Savannah! The only way we can be captured is if we were attacked by land through the swamps!"

The boys and Lucky hurried back to the ship's boat and were returned to the AMERICAN DREAM, where they reported that the Patriots controlled Savannah.

"I still have grave concerns that there is something being planned by the British," Captain Richards pondered. He added, "We will go to Savannah, celebrate Christmas, and quickly return to sea. I fear the British have designs on Savannah and we want no part of it."

Christmas morning dawned with a chill in the air. The AMERICAN DREAM, and the French merchant ship both flew the Stars and Stripes high upon their masts as they sailed by the stately Tybee Island Lighthouse. Angel, with a flourish of flippers, remained swimming back and forth near the mouth of the river. Soon the ships passed the little mounds of sod that composed Mud Fort. With a wave at the soldiers who were expecting them, they then sailed into Savannah.

The sun broke through the clouds and was

shining brightly as the citizens of Savannah, in their Sunday best, were on their way from church. They stopped to watch and wave excitedly to welcome the two ships tying up along River Street. The British blockade had been so successful that the appearance of these ships was a miracle on this Christmas Day.

Gathering the entire crew on deck, Captain Richards proudly announced, "Each of you may go on board the French merchant ship and take an equal share of the cargo to give as gifts to the citizens of Savannah this Christmas Day. You can act as St. Nicholas, or Sinter Klaas, if you like."

"What do you mean?" James asked the smiling Captain.

"According to the legend, St. Nicholas arrived on the eve of St. Nicholas and left gifts for the people," Captain Richards replied. "Now all of us have the opportunity to understand the meaning of Christmas by giving gifts and love without expecting anything in return. We will save the Christmas spirit by bringing the joy of the season to this suffering city."

"When do you want us back on board?" Samuel asked anxiously, hoping for as much time on shore as possible.

"I feel the British are up to something, so we shall sail shortly after sunset tonight," Captain Richards replied. Then, breaking into a large grin, he exclaimed, "I want to wish each of you the merriest time on shore and a wonderful holiday. You can all celebrate in your own way."

James noticed Solomon Friedman, a Jewish crewmember, and asked, "What are you planning for this holiday?"

"I shall take my share of the cargo and go to visit the Temple Mickve Israel," Solomon replied.

Samuel, who also wanted this Christmas to be special for all, looked at Lt. Jackson, the large dark-skinned man who had become one of his heroes.

"Don't worry Samuel," Lt. Jackson began and then explained, "Savannah is a good place for me to spend Christmas. The other black sailors and I plan to take our shares of the cargo to the First African Baptist Church where George Leile is the pastor. We will have a wonderful Christmas."

"How about you, Mr. Lugo?" James questioned.

"Aye, son, there is an inn close by that has the reputation for the best grog and food a sailor can hope for," Lugo laughed. "Where better to spend a holiday than a cozy inn that caters to the likes of pirates and sailors!"

When they were satisfied that all of their shipmates would have a merry Christmas, James and Samuel began to plan their day.

"Here are some bags. Let's go fill them with gifts so we can go ashore," Samuel told James.

"Can't I go along?" Sarah begged as she overheard them. There was a pleading look in her eyes. "First, though, my mother has insisted that we stay together for a Christmas dinner before

57

we go on our own. I believe the Captain is escorting us to a private room at the inn."

"Why certainly," James quickly answered with the memory of yesterday's kiss on the cheek fresh in his mind. The three then hurried below deck to fill the bags with gifts to be handed out later that day.

At the inn, the cheerful group was first served "hush puppies" and hungrily ate them as fast as the servers brought them to the table.

As they ate, Louise told them how "hush puppies" got their name. "The dogs used to bark outside the back door of the kitchen when they smelled the food that the cook was preparing. She would fry small pieces of bread and throw some to the dogs to keep them quiet. At the same time she would yell, 'hush puppies' to try to quiet them down."

After the festive dinner, Louise told the others that she had managed to find a couple that would take Sarah and her to Charles Town in return for lodging at her brother's home.

Christmas afternoon passed delightfully as the ship's crewmembers distributed gifts throughout the city. James, Samuel, and Sarah went back to the ship to get Lucky. They then joined a group of hearty sailors who, as children, had been orphans, and they all took their bags of toys to the Bethesda Home for Boys. The expressions of joy on the orphans' faces as they saw the tops, lead toy soldiers, and games were unforgettable. It was the happiest and most wonderful Christmas many had ever spent; a glorious day of sharing!

The early evening sunset was spectacular, with golden rays shining on puffy clouds and tinting them a brilliant pink.

The townspeople, joining with sailors from the ship, gathered on the cobblestone River Street to say their farewells. When Sarah appeared at the bow of the AMERICAN DREAM with her violin, Samuel was at her side with his drum and other sailors appeared with a variety of instruments. As they began to play beloved Christmas carols, the grateful voices of the townspeople joined their melody.

As the sun finished setting, candles were passed around and the celebration of song continued. Finally, the darkness and oncoming chill of the night brought an end to the very special Christmas Day.

It was with regret that the crew of the AMERICAN DREAM made final preparations to leave their newly found friends.

James stopped on the gangplank, turned, and waved to the crowd. When Sarah and her mother came up to him, Sarah whispered, "You have made this the best Christmas of my life and I am going to miss you. Promise that you will come back and find me." With that, she turned, ran off the ship, and into the crowd ashore.

The dock lines were cast from the ship and as the brigantine began to sail down the Savannah River, the large crowd sang "Joy to the World".

As the ship passed down the moonlit river and through the glow of the Tybee Island lighthouse, Captain Richards ordered more sail.

Lucky was at her post on the bow as she listened for the slapping sounds of Angel's flukes on the water guiding the ship into open seas.

The next morning at sunrise, the lookout cried out, "On the horizon, more British ships than I have ever seen!"

Fully alert now, Captain Richards ordered the **AMERICAN DREAM** to full battle stations and the crew frantically battened down as they prepared for a deadly barrage from the enormous fleet.

The attack never happened. There was an eerie silence as the British fleet stayed at anchor and watched the American privateer ship sail by them toward Florida.

"I don't understand why they didn't attack us," Lt. Jackson exclaimed.

"They can only have a bigger plan and a more important target. I fear for the citizens of Savannah. We can best help the cause now by escaping and fighting the British another day," Captain Richards sadly replied.

"You know, we did do something for them," Lt. Jackson continued. "We gave them a Christmas they will never forget in spite of anything that is coming. Regardless of events, we must always remember the importance of loving and giving at Christmas."

Savannah was captured by the British three days later on December 29, 1778.

EPILOGUE

An epilogue tells us what happened to some of the main characters in the novel.

CAPTAIN RICHARDS

Continued as captain of **AMERICAN DREAM** until the end of the Revolutionary War. He became famous for landing troops on shore to capture territory or win battles. Following the war, Captain Richards became a United States Navy Officer. He supported the formation of the United States Marine Corps that first fought against the Barbary Pirates on the shores of Tripoli. He married Louise Melbourne and they had two sons.

LT. MOSES JACKSON

After serving heroically until the end of the Revolutionary War, Lt. Jackson returned to the Carolinas where he established schools for freed Black slaves. He became an outspoken leader for the equality of Black Americans.

JAMES HUNTER

After the war, along with Captain Richards, he joined the United States Navy and was commissioned an officer. He served as Captain of one of the most famous ships fighting against the Barbary Pirates. James married Sarah and they had four children, all accomplished musicians. They had a large house on Tybee Island.

SAMUEL REED

After his service in the war, Samuel returned to Key West, Florida. Along with a number of other inventors and environmentalists, he was responsible for numerous inventions that both benefited the shipping industry and protected the fragile chain of keys. Samuel married an opera singer and had three children.

LUCKY

Served along with all the others aboard the **AMERICAN DREAM** through the end of the war. She then served on the U.S. Navy ship commanded by Captain Richards until she died on board in 1787. Lucky was given a full Navy funeral with a sunset burial at sea off Key West, Florida. Many an old sailor swears to this day that; if you look into the many colorful sunsets off Key West, you may see a beautiful white dolphin jumping from the water with a brown, tan and black dog happily barking while riding on its back.

GLOSSARY

AFT – the back or stern of a vessel or ship.

AHOY – a call used in hailing or calling out to a ship.

ANCHOR – a heavy object, usually made of iron, shaped with flukes and attached to a chain and lowered into the water to keep a ship from drifting.

ARTICLES – (Articles of Confederation) is a contract signed by pirates before going on a voyage. The articles are the ship's rules and how each person will be paid or divide up any prize or booty.

AVAST – simply means to "stop."

BAR OR SANDBAR – a sandbank or a shoal, often under shallow water, at the mouth of a harbor, bay, or sound.

BLOCKADE – shutting off of a port or city to prevent anyone from getting in or out.

BOOTY – a prize or cargo taken from a captured or sunken ship.

BOW – the front part of a ship or boat.

BOWSPRIT – a heavy spar that points forward from the bow of a ship.

BRIGANTINE – a two-masted sailing vessel that can be rigged with either square or fore and aft sails. Generally a shallow draft hulled vessel that could sail in shallow or deep waters avoiding capture.

BROADSIDE – (two definitions in this book) 1. The simultaneous firing of all the cannons on one side of a ship at an enemy, 2. A large sheet of paper printed on one side and used to convey a political message or news, often posted on poles, trees, and bulletin boards.

CAREEN – to intentionally beach a ship, lay it over and remove the barnacles and seaweed from the hull.

COBBLESTONE – a rounded stone used as ballast in sailing ships and for paving streets.

COLORS – the flags flown on ships to show what country they come from.

COWBOYS – a term given to the colonists who remained loyal to England for the way in which they robbed or stole livestock from the 'rebels' or colonists fighting against England. The valuables taken or the livestock were sold or given to the British Army.

DOUBLOON – a gold Spanish coin.

FATHOM – a measure of six feet in length used to define the depth of water.

FLUKES – on dolphins, two adjacent horizontal flat appendages act like a paddle propelling the dolphin through the water with every up and down flex of the tail muscle.

FORE – the front part of a ship at the bow.

FORECASTLE – the upper deck of a ship in front of the foremast.

FRIGATE – a fast, three masted square rigged navy ship carrying between 24 and 40 cannons.

GALLEY – the kitchen of a ship.

GANGPLANK – a moveable bridge used in boarding or leaving a ship at a pier or dock.

HULL – the frame or body of a ship, without sails or rigging.

JOLLY ROGER – A pirate ship's flag. Can have either a red or black background with symbols of death, like a skull and crossbones.

LETTER OF MARQUE – a contract, license, or a commission issued by a government authorizing private vessels to attack and capture all ships of an enemy nation.

LONGBOAT (SHIP'S BOAT) – Generally the largest boat belonging to a ship that is used to carry heavy items and crewmembers to and from the ship.

LOYALIST (TORIES) – an American colonist upholding the cause of the British crown or remaining loyal to England during the American Revolution.

MAN-OF-WAR – an armed warship, generally a large one, used by the navy of a country with a national navy.

MERCHANT VESSEL (Merchantman)– a ship that transports goods and items used in commerce.

PATRIOTS (REBELS) – During the American Revolution, those colonists who declared their independence from England and fought to form a new United States of America.

PIECE OF EIGHT – a Spanish coin used throughout the American colonies during the time of the American Revolution. Actually was our first currency.

PIRATES – men and women who loved freedom and robbed and plundered at sea and land to earn a living. They believed in democracy and equality.

POD – a group of dolphins that live together.

PORT – the left side of a ship as you face forward toward the bow.

PRIVATEERS – Armed privately owned ships, including the captain and crew, authorized by a commission or "Letter of Marque" by one country to attack and capture ships of an enemy country.

QUARTERDECK – a deck above the main deck at the stern (back) of the ship from where the captain and other officers control the ship.

RATLINE – ropes forming the steps of a series of rope ladders running from the hull of a ship up the different masts.

RIGGING – the arrangement of sails and masts on a ship.

SCUTTLE – to sink or attempt to sink a ship by cutting a hole in the hull.

SQUADRON – a naval unit consisting of two or more divisions and sometimes additional vessels.

SQUARE RIGGED – sails set at right angles from horizontal yards attached to a mast of a ship.

STARBOARD – the right side of a ship as you face forward toward the bow.

STERN – the rear or back of a ship or boat.

SWIVEL GUN – a small cannon that is mounted on a swivel, and mounted on the rail or from the fighting tops of vessels.

SWEET TRADE – the name given to the practice of piracy, one of the oldest professions in all the world.

YARD – a long spar (wood) suspended from the mast of a ship to extend the sails.

OTHER PIRATE BOOKS
BY

THE KASERMANS

Available at online book sites or at bookstores worldwide.